You Are Sailing Up to the Sky on Your Magic Carpet!

Whee! You love to make circles and squares and loops!

You love flying!

You fly toward the clouds.

You go in and out of the clouds and all around the poofy shapes. Far in the distance you see a beautiful cloud city.

Below you is a mysterious dark cloud.

If you fly to the cloud city, turn to page 8.

If you explore the dark cloud, turn to page 10.

**WHAT WILL HAPPEN NEXT?
TURN THE PAGE FOR
MORE THRILLS AND FUN!
WHATEVER YOU DO,
IT'S UP TO YOU!**

WHICH WAY SECRET DOOR Books for you to enjoy

Available from ARCHWAY paperbacks

which way · secret door · books

#7

R.G. Austin

The Magic Carpet

Illustrated by
Winslow Pels

AN ARCHWAY PAPERBACK
Published by POCKET BOOKS · NEW YORK

For Reggie and Jack

AN ARCHWAY PAPERBACK *Original*

 An Archway Paperback published by
POCKET BOOKS, a division of Simon & Schuster, Inc.
1230 Avenue of the Americas, New York, N.Y. 10020

ISBN: 0-671-47568-1

First Archway Paperback printing November, 1983

10 9 8 7 6 5 4 3 2 1

AN ARCHWAY PAPERBACK and colophon are
trademarks of Simon & Schuster, Inc.

WHICH WAY is a registered trademark
of Simon & Schuster, Inc.

SECRET DOOR is a trademark
of Simon & Schuster, Inc.

Printed in the U.S.A.

IL 1+

ATTENTION!

READING A SECRET DOOR BOOK
IS LIKE PLAYING A GAME.

HERE ARE THE RULES

Begin reading on page 1. When you come to a choice, decide what to do and follow the directions. Keep reading and following the directions until you come to an ending. Then go back to the beginning and make new choices.

There are many stories and many endings in this book.

HAVE FUN!

It is dark outside. You have gone to bed, but you are still wide awake.

You lie quietly until everyone in the house is asleep. Then you creep out of bed and tiptoe into the closet.

You push away the clothes and knock three times on the back wall. Soon the secret door begins to move. It opens just wide enough for you to slip through.

Turn to page 2.

You step into a large room. In the middle of the floor is a thick, furry rug. You love soft, fuzzy rugs, so you sit down on it.

Suddenly the rug begins to move! Then it lifts you off the ground and flies out the window.

You are riding on a magic carpet!

If you want to go into town to show off your new carpet, turn to page 4.

If you want to take a spin in the sky, turn to page 6.

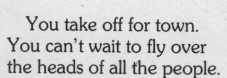

You take off for town.
You can't wait to fly over
the heads of all the people.

At the edge of the town is a
large park. As you are flying over,
the children shout and wave at you.
You wave back.

You decide to land your carpet in the
playground. You lean forward, tipping
the front of the carpet down.

Soon you are standing in the middle of a
swarm of excited children.

All day long you give them free rides on
the carpet. Finally, you are exhausted. You
tell the children that you are going home but
that you will be back the next day.

At home, you have a wonderful idea.

Turn to page 40.

You lean back and point the carpet up. Soon you are sailing into the sky.

Whee! You make circles and squares and loops.

You love flying!

You fly toward the clouds.

You go in and out of the clouds and all around the poofy shapes. Far in the distance you see a beautiful cloud city.

Below you is a big, mysterious, dark cloud.

If you fly to the cloud city, turn to page 8.

If you explore the dark cloud, turn to page 10.

You fly toward the city. As you get closer you see towers and buildings and soft white mountains.

In front of you is a fabulous castle. You sail right through a large window.

Inside, you hear music. You land your carpet and begin to explore.

If you follow the music, turn to page 12.

If you go up the stairs to the tower, turn to page 15.

You head for the
cloud. You like the idea
of exploring the
unknown.
You enter the cloud.
It is dark and scary in there.
You steer to the right, then to
the left, searching for a speck of light.
Suddenly you feel a terrible thud! Then
Crash! Bang!
You fall off your carpet!
You think maybe the carpet is circling
above you. But you also feel something flut-
tering right in front of you.

If you reach up for the carpet, turn to
page 36.

If you reach for the object in front of
you, turn to page 38.

You listen to the music as you walk through the dining room and down a long, long hallway. The music grows louder.

You enter the ballroom. Inside, there are hundreds of tiny people dancing. They are having a wonderful time.

Suddenly the room begins to shake.

"It's the giant!" someone yells. "Quick! Hide before he finds us!"

"I can't hide," you say. "I have to go back and get my carpet. The giant might steal it."

"Well, watch out," says a voice. "That giant is mean."

You are scared, but you have to get your carpet.

Turn to page 16.

You dash up the stairs, going around and around as you go higher in the tower.

When you get to the very top of the tower, you come to a door. There is a big sign on the door that says, "RAINBOW ROOM."

You knock on the door, but there is no answer. You can hear voices inside. As you stand there, the voices grow louder and louder. There is an argument going on inside the Rainbow Room.

Turn to page 18.

You run back to get your carpet. Just as you enter the room where you left it, you see a huge giant. He leans down and picks up your carpet.

"A magic carpet!" the giant booms. "I'm so lucky to find it."

If you think you should tell the giant that the carpet belongs to you, turn to page 21.

If you hide and see what the giant plans to do with the carpet, turn to page 22.

You open the door a crack. Now you can hear the voices clearly.

"It's my turn to do the red," says one voice.

"No, it's not! You did red yesterday! It's my turn."

"Well, I'm doing yellow today," says a third voice. "You guys better make up your minds. We have work to do."

You are looking at one of the strangest sights you have ever seen. Inside the room are five little elves. They are dipping long strips of silk into pots of brightly colored paint.

And then they are taking the strips and pushing them out the window. You can see a long streamer of colors reaching across the sky.

Oh, wow! you think. *This is the place where rainbows are made!*

As you stand there, the elves' argument grows louder and louder.

"Well, I think we should just mix all the colors together. It's easier that way!" says one elf.

If you try to stop the elves from mixing all the colors together, turn to page 28.

If you think you should stay out of the argument, turn to page 31.

"Hey, you up there!" you yell.

"Did I hear a mouse?" roars the giant.

"No! It's me!" you yell.

The giant looks down. "What do you want?" he asks.

"That's my carpet!"

"It's mine now. Finders keepers, losers weepers," he says.

You don't know what to do. The giant is too big to fight. You try to think of an idea.

If you offer to flip a coin for the carpet, turn to page 25.

If you try to tickle the giant, turn to page 27.

You watch as the giant sits down on the carpet. He is so huge that he flops over the edges.

You can see the carpet trying to take off. It flutters and wiggles and tries its best. But the giant is just too heavy.

"You sure are a second-rate carpet," the giant yells. "You're defective!"

The giant gets very angry!

Finally the giant gets so angry at the carpet that he throws it into the trash can. Then he stomps out of the room, shaking the whole castle as he goes.

You pick up the carpet and run to the ballroom.

"You got rid of the giant!" the little people yell. "You're a hero!"

"Come on!" you say. "Let's celebrate! Free rides for everybody!"

The End

"That carpet belongs to me," you yell to the giant. "But if you think it belongs to you, then at least flip a coin for it."

"Flip a coin?" says the giant.

"Yes," you yell.

"All right," the giant agrees.

"Heads I win, tails you lose. OK?" you ask.

"OK," the giant says.

You flip the coin. It is tails.

"You lose," you tell the giant.

"Darn!" he says as he gives you the carpet.

Quickly, you hop on the carpet, fly out the window and head for home.

That was a pretty smart solution!

The End

You hop onto the giant's sneaker and climb up the laces. Then you lean over the top of his foot and put your hand inside his shoe.

P.U.! you think. *What an awful smell.* You tickle the bottom of his foot.

"Ho, ho, ho, ha, ha!" the giant laughs. He wiggles all over. He throws up his hands and flings the carpet into the air.

Then he wiggles his toes and kicks his foot. You fly into the air!

I'm going to crash! you think. Just as you are about to slam into the wall, the carpet sails under you.

You grab hold of the carpet and hang on. Once you get your balance, you sail once around the angry giant's head. Then the carpet flies through the window and you head for home.

The End

"Hey!" you shout. "You're going to make an ugly rainbow if you mix all those colors together."

"What do you mean?" the elves ask.

"If you put all your colors into one pot, you'll end up with black paint."

"We don't want that!" the elves shout. "This is only our second day on the job. Can you show us how to mix colors? Let's make a purple rainbow!"

If you think you can get purple by mixing blue and yellow, turn to page 32.

If you think you can get purple by mixing red and blue, turn to page 34.

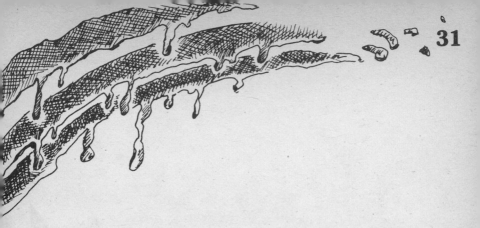

You decide to stay out of the argument.

The elves scream at each other. Then they begin to throw paint. Soon they are dumping the colors on the floor and dipping the silk into the ugly mixture.

When you see what is happening, you try to stop them. But it is too late.

"Look!" you yell at them. "See what your fighting has done. That's the ugliest rainbow I've seen in my whole life!"

Everyone looks out the window. There, streaking across the sky, is a black and gray and brown rainbow. Yuck.

The End

You pour the blue and yellow paint into one big pot. The elves stir it very carefully.

Much to your disappointment, the mixture turns green instead of purple.

"Oh, well," says one of the elves, "I guess it's not too bad to have a green rainbow." And they start to dip the silk.

"It's sort of pretty," you say when you see the green streaming across the sky. "At least it's better than a black rainbow."

The End

Everybody works together. The elves take the red paint and pour it into the bucket of blue paint. When they stir it, the paint turns purple. Then they dip the silk in the paint.

Soon there is a dark purple streamer floating across the sky. Then you take some white and mix it into the purple. The paint turns light purple. You and the elves make another streamer.

You keep adding new streamers of different shades of purple.

When you are finished, you stand with the elves at the window and admire your work. You think that this is surely the most beautiful rainbow in the world.

The End

You reach up
and grab a piece
of fringe. Then you
swing your legs onto
            the carpet.
    Whew! you think. *That
was a close call. I'd better get
out of this cloud.*
    You start to fly to your left, but
you do not come out of the cloud.
There seems to be no end to it. You
change directions, but still you are caught
in this murky darkness.
    Suddenly you begin to spin.
    You turn slowly at first. Then you spin faster and faster.
    Oh, no! you think. *I'm caught in a tornado!*

If you try to fly down, turn to page 52.

If you try to fly up, turn to page 54.

You reach out and
grab hold of something.
I don't know what it is, you think, *but I'd
better climb up on this thing. It's better
than falling through the sky.*

You climb on and begin to fly. Suddenly
you burst out of the cloud into the sunlight.

You discover that you are riding on the back of the most beautiful white horse you have ever seen. And the horse has wings!

"My name is Pegasus," the horse says.

You explain about losing your carpet.

"I can take you to look for it," Pegasus says. "Or, if you wish, you can fly with me to the highest cloud in the sky."

If you go in search of the carpet, turn to page 51.

If you fly to the highest cloud with Pegasus, turn to page 53.

You wake up early and make a big sign. Then you get on your carpet and fly to the park. You set up your sign:

CARPET RIDES—$1.00

Soon the children come. They wait in line for their turns.

You sit at the back of the carpet and call the first rider. She hands you a dollar and climbs on.

You wait for the carpet to fly, but it does not budge.

"Come on, carpet . . . fly!" you say. But the carpet stays right on the ground.

"Maybe the carpet doesn't like to work for money," a kid suggests.

"Yeah," says another. "Magic should be free."

If you give the rider her dollar back but take her for a ride anyway, turn to page 42.

If you trick the carpet by collecting the money at the end of the day, turn to page 46.

If you give up on rides and fly off on your carpet, turn to page 50.

You give the dollar back. As soon as you do, the carpet takes off. *The magic only works for free,* you think. *Oh, well . . . that's the way it goes.*

You and your passenger have a wonderful ride.

"I've never had so much fun in my whole life," your passenger tells you.

When you get back to the playground, all the children are shouting that they want their turns. You tell them to wait in line.

Then a great big kid pushes to the front of the line. He puts his hands on his hips and tells you, "It's my turn next. And you better give it to me."

This kid is obviously a bully.

If you give the bully the next ride, turn to page 44.

If you refuse to give the bully the next ride, turn to page 48.

You don't want to take the bully for a ride. But he threatens to cut up your carpet, so you agree to give him a ride.

The bully climbs onto the carpet with you and it takes off. When you are over the lake, the bully turns to you and says, "This is where you get off."

Then he tries to push you off the carpet. You hang on. He is still pushing when the carpet flies over a farm.

You are flying over a big pile of cow manure when the carpet tips suddenly, and the bully falls off.

He lands in the middle of the pile!

You can't wait to get back to the park to tell all the kids what happened. You know they will be as happy as you are.

The End

You give rides to the children all day long.

And you make them promise to pay you at the end of the day.

Everybody rides. Fifty-six kids in all. *That's fifty-six dollars!* you think. *Just imagine if I do this every day! I'll be rich!*

At the end of the day, the children pay you for their rides. You have fifty-six dollars! You can't wait to ride home and show your family. You sure have tricked that carpet!

As you collect your last dollar, someone shouts, "LOOK!"

You turn just in time to see your carpet fly away.

That carpet is smarter than I thought, you think.

You would rather have the magic than the money. But it's too late now.

The End

You tell the bully to go to the end of the line and wait for his turn. But this bully doesn't like that suggestion of yours.

He pushes you off the carpet and he jumps on. The carpet takes off!

"Nyah, nyah, nyah!" the bully sneers as he rides away. "The carpet's mine now."

You are so upset that you begin to cry. All the kids try to comfort you. But it does no good.

You are certain that you will never see your carpet again.

In about ten minutes, the empty carpet lands right in front of you!

"Hooray!" everyone shouts. "The carpet has come home!"

A few minutes later, the bully comes into the playground. He is soaking wet.

"That stupid carpet dumped me in the lake," he grumbles. "I didn't like that crummy old toy anyway."

You look forward to all the fun you and the children are going to have with that crummy old toy.

The End

You are flying over a tree a few blocks from the park when you hear a tiny "Meow."

You look down. You see a kitten stuck in a tree.

"Meow, meow, meow."

If you try a flying rescue, turn to page 55.

If you land your carpet and climb up the tree, turn to page 56.

You fly all around the black cloud.

When you get to the very bottom, you see the carpet flying just ahead of you.

"There it is!" you shout.

Pegasus chases the carpet. In just a few minutes, he is flying alongside the carpet. Very carefully, you climb from the back of Pegasus onto the carpet.

"I must go now," Pegasus says. He tips his wings once in your direction.

You watch this incredible creature fly toward the sun. His shining brightness is the most beautiful sight you have ever seen.

You are happy that you have your carpet back. But you will always wonder what was in the highest cloud.

The End

You aim your carpet down. Faster and faster you spin.

When you get to the bottom, you can see that the tornado is traveling over the flat countryside.

Just as you reach the ground, the tornado rises. It drops you gently in a field of clover.

I'm probably the only person on earth who has ridden down the center of a tornado, you think. But you wonder if anyone will believe you when you tell them about it.

The End

You wave good-bye to your carpet. Then you fly with Pegasus to the highest cloud in the sky. Hundreds of rainbows form arches above the cloud. Stars twinkle in the distance. Even the rain is soft and warm.

Pegasus takes you to his sky home and introduces you to his friends. You talk to a unicorn. You swim with mermaids. You touch the stars.

This is the most perfect day of your life.

The End

You fly up, right through the center of the tornado.

Suddenly you burst out of the twisting cloud into a clear blue sky.

That was really a close call, you think. *I think I'll go home now.*

And you fly off back to earth.

The End

If you want to stay in the sky, you can go explore the cloud city on page 8.

You fly close to the tree. Then you guide the carpet between the branches.

Oops! The carpet gets caught on a limb. As you try to untangle it, some of the fringe gets caught in the branches. The harder you work, the more tangled the carpet gets. You are hopelessly stuck.

Now the fire department is going to have to rescue the kitten *and* you.

But first you have to let them know that you're stuck.

"Help!" you shout.

"Meow!"

"Help! Help!"

"Meow! Meow!"

"Help! Help! Help!"

"Meow! Meow! Meow!"

The End

You land your carpet near the trunk of the tree. Then you start to climb.

You get to the branch where the kitten is stuck and you lean out. Just as you get a firm grip on the kitten, you lose your balance.

You are falling! You hold onto the kitten and hope you don't break a leg when you crash.

Suddenly you feel something soft under you. The carpet has flown up to catch you!

You have saved the kitten. And the carpet has saved you. You and the carpet are both heroes!

The End

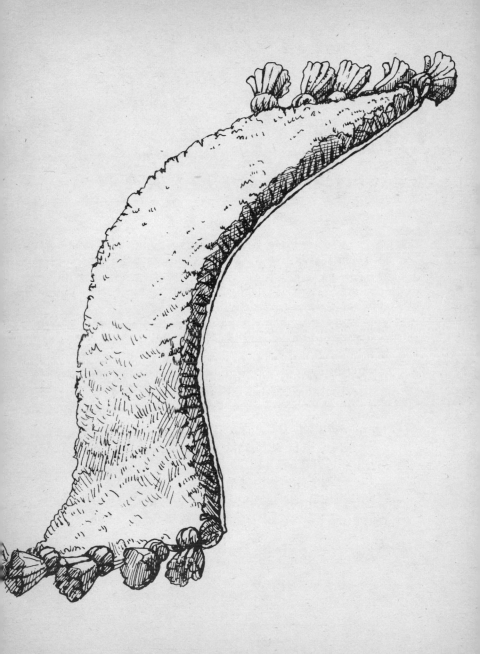

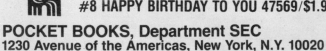